This book
belongs to

.........................................

# Puddle's Fan Pages

Here's what other children have to say about their favourite puppy and his latest adventure!

"Puddle is very funny and a cheeky puppy." Isobel, age 6

"This was a funny book and made me laugh. Puddle was naughty but helped save the day! I loved the bit when they jumped through the puddle." Abby, age 5

"I liked Puddle because he was so clever and also because he was magic. I liked it when he found the wand especially. I liked Simon's stutter and that he was a bit clumsy (like me!). I think Ruby had light brown hair like mine and she wore it in plaits." Evie, age 5

"There's lots of magic – and it's funny. One funny bit was when Simon's wand fell into the water. But most funny was when Simon thought a string of sausages was a snake." Alice, age 7

"My favourite bits were when they fell into the puddle and met Simon the wizard-in-training. And when everyone did their acts in the magic show, especially when Simon made the sausages disappear, with Puddle's help!" Daisy, age 6

# Magic Mayhem

**Other books about
Puddle the Naughtiest Puppy:**

Magic Carpet Ride

Toyshop Trouble

Ballet Show Mischief

Rainforest Hide and Seek

Dragon Dance

# Puddle
## the naughtiest puppy

# Magic Mayhem

by Hayley Daze
illustrated by David Opie
cover illustrated by Paul Hardman

A catalogue record for this book is available from the British Library

Published by Ladybird Books Ltd  MMX
A Penguin Company
Penguin Books Ltd., 80 Strand, London WC2R 0RL, UK
Penguin Books Australia Ltd., Camberwell, Victoria, Australia
Penguin Group (NZ) 67 Apollo Drive, Rosedale,
North Shore 0632, New Zealand

3

Series created by Working Partners Limited, London WC1X 9HH
Text © Working Partners Ltd MMX
Cover illustration © Working Partners Ltd MMX
Interior illustrations © Ladybird Books Ltd MMX

*Special thanks to Jane Clarke*

ISBN: 978-1-40930-332-9

**Mixed Sources**
Product group from well-managed
forests and other controlled sources
www.fsc.org   Cert no. SA-COC-001592
© 1996 Forest Stewardship Council

FSC

*For James and Victoria*

When clouds fill the sky and rain starts to fall,
Ruby and Harry are not sad at all.
They know that when puddles appear on the ground,
A magical puppy will soon be around!

Puddle's his name, and he's the one
Who can lead you to worlds of adventure and fun!
He may be quite naughty, but he's clever too,
So come follow Puddle – he's waiting for you!

A present from Puddle:

Look out for the special code at the back of the book to
get extra-special games and loads of free stuff at Puddle's
website! Come and play at www.puddlethepuppy.com

# Contents

# Chapter One
# The Magic Begins

"It's time for the magic show to start!" Ruby announced. Her long plaits swung to and fro as she waved the glittery magic wand she'd made out of a wooden spoon covered in silver tinsel.

Ruby and her cousin Harry were sitting on the carpet in the lounge of Grandad's cottage, wearing home-made wizard hats. Ruby had stuck little silver stars all over the dark blue paper cones and they twinkled in the darkened room.

"I'm not ready," Harry told Ruby. He pushed his glasses up his nose. "I have to consult my *Big Book of Magic Tricks*," he said. "And I can't see it properly because you closed the curtains."

"Magic shows always happen in the dark," Ruby said. "Watch me use my Hocus-Pocus Plaits to make Grandad's last biscuit disappear like magic. *Abracadabra!*" Ruby tugged on her plaits for luck, then waved her wand so it knocked Harry's

wizard hat down over his glasses. She
popped the biscuit into her mouth.

"*Ta-da!*" Ruby spluttered, with her
mouth full of crumbs. She pointed to
the empty plate.

"That wasn't real magic," Harry said, as he rearranged his hat. "I'll show you a real magic trick." He picked up a marble and a paper cup.

"Watch."

Harry held the paper cup in the palm of his hand and dropped the marble inside it. He looked at Ruby over the top of his glasses.

"*Hey presto!*" he said, waving his free hand over the paper cup. He turned it upside down.

It was empty. The marble had disappeared!

"That's amazing!" Ruby exclaimed as Harry set the cup back down on the carpet. "How did you do that?"

"I made a hole in the bottom of the cup, just like the book told me to," Harry said. "The marble's still in my hand! The next part of the trick is to make the audience believe I've magicked it somewhere else . . . *Hey presto!*" Harry pretended to pull the marble out of one of Ruby's plaits.

"You're a great magician, Hey Presto Harry!" Ruby giggled. "But magicians are supposed to keep their tricks secret."

All at once a breeze swirled through the room, making the curtains flap and billow. A little bundle of fur bounded into the lounge, with a joyful, "Woof!"

"Puddle, you're back!" Ruby gasped.

He crashed into them. *Whump!* Harry's hat and paper cup and Ruby's hat and magic wand were sent flying across the carpet.

Ruby scooped up their naughty little puppy friend and gave him an enormous cuddly hug. Puddle's tail wagged as he licked her face.

Harry pulled back the curtains. Raindrops were pitter-pattering

against the windows. Ruby and
Harry beamed at each other.
Whenever it rained, Puddle arrived
and they went on amazing adventures
together!

Puddle squirmed out of Ruby's arms and ran to the front door, yapping excitedly. Ruby and Harry quickly pulled on their wellies. The instant the door was open, Puddle scampered outside, splishing and sploshing through the puddles on the path.

"Woof!" Puddle skidded to a halt in front of a huge puddle that glimmered and shimmered like a mirror.

Ruby smiled with delight as Puddle began to race around it, wagging his wet tail. With a great leap, the little puppy jumped into the puddle – and, in a rainbow of water drops, he disappeared from view!

Ruby could feel excitement fizzing up from the tips of her toes to the ends of her plaits.

"Quick! Follow that puppy!" she told Harry. "One ... two ... three – *JUMP!*"

And with a humongous splash Ruby and Harry leapt into the puddle. Another magical adventure was about to begin!

# Chapter Two
# Puddle Trouble

Ruby opened her eyes. All around her were high stone walls with battlements and towers.

Just in time, she jumped out of the way as three knights in shining armour clip-clopped past her on gleaming chestnut horses. She was in the courtyard of a castle! There were ladies wearing beautiful silk gowns

and tall pointy hats, and men and
boys in brightly coloured tunics and
tights. They were dashing to and
fro, carrying trays piled high with

pastries, pies and towering wobbly
jellies. Ruby thought they were
preparing for some kind of party.

But there was no sign of Harry or Puddle.

Ruby looked around, puzzled. Behind her, a big haystack propped against the castle wall began to shudder. Ruby held her breath as she watched it twitch and heave. A muffled bark and sneeze came from deep within it.

"Harry! Puddle! Come out of there!" Ruby called, diving head first into the dusty hay. She dug among the haystack until Harry's head emerged.

"*Atchoo!*" Harry sneezed. He pushed his glasses back on to his nose and scrambled out, looking like a

walking scarecrow. His mouth fell
open as he saw where he was.

"We're in a medieval castle," he
gasped. "It's just like the one in my
history book."

There was a muffled, "Woof!" and
Puddle burst out of the haystack in
an explosion of hay.

"Good to see you again," Ruby laughed. "Let's explore! But don't get into trouble, Puddle."

A man with a basket full of sausages hurried past the haystack. A long string of sausages trailed out of the basket and was dragging along the ground. Puddle sniffed the air. His ears pricked up, and with a happy, "yip, yip, yip," he bounded after them.

"Puddle, come back!" Ruby called. But it was no good. The little puppy was darting between the legs of the knights' horses, trying to grab at the string of sausages.

"He's being naughty again," Harry groaned, as the horses reared up in alarm. One knight's helmet fell off as he struggled to control his horse.

"Come on!" said Ruby, dashing off after Puddle. They zigzagged their way across the crowded castle courtyard. A flock of chickens stopped pecking at the dirt and began flapping and *pock-pock-pocking*. Puddle and the man with the sausage basket were heading for the gatehouse. Ruby could see them hurrying past a wobbly pile of wooden trestle tables and benches piled up against the side of the gatehouse. Right next to them was a giant catapult.

Then suddenly the man with the basket turned into a doorway in the gatehouse, making the string of

sausages sweep through the air.
Puddle launched himself at them.

The door shut with a slam, sending
Puddle flying!

"Uh-oh," said Harry, covering his
eyes.

# Chapter Three
# Wizard-in-Waiting

Puddle landed on the wobbly pile of benches and tables. As they began to fall, the naughty puppy jumped on to a boy who was passing by.

"Look out!" called Ruby. The boy was wearing a blue wizard's hat and flowing robes covered with big gold stars.

Puddle landed on the boy's hat.

The hat and the naughty little puppy
tumbled into his arms.

"It's r-raining hats and d-dogs!"
the boy exclaimed, looking up at the
sky.

"That's Puddle," Ruby said. "I'm
Ruby and this is my cousin Harry.
We're very sorry about your hat."

"It's always
getting c-c-
crumpled."
The boy
laughed. "L-let
me introduce
myself." He put
Puddle down
and bowed low,

knocking down a table as he did so.

"W-whoops!" he said, as the table clattered to the ground.

"Hello, Whoops," said Ruby. "It's lovely to meet a real wizard!"

The boy grinned. "My name's not W-Whoops," he said. "It's Simon. And I'm not a real w-wizard. I'm wizard-in-training to the G-Great Magnifico!" Simon's hat fell off again as he tried to put it back on.

"Whoops!" he laughed.

Puddle caught the hat in his teeth.

"Thanks, P-Puddle," Simon said with a smile as he plonked his hat back on his head. Puddle's tooth marks dotted the rim. "W-want to hear a p-puppy joke?" he asked Ruby, Harry and Puddle hopefully.

They nodded.

"H-how do you find your puppy if he's lost in the woods?" Simon asked.

They all shook their heads. Simon's eyes twinkled. "Put your ear up to a tree and listen for the bark!"

He put a hand to his ear as if he were listening, knocking over a chair as he did so.

"That's a great joke!" Ruby giggled.

"What are all these tables for?" Harry asked as he helped Simon pick up the one he and Puddle had knocked over.

"They're for the queen's b-birthday party," Simon explained. "It's later today, and I'm not ready. I don't think I'll ever be ready to be a w-wizard," he said with a frown.

"What's the matter?" Ruby asked. "Perhaps we can help."

"The G-Great Magnifico is poorly," Simon said. "So I have to do the m-magic show."

"That sounds like fun." Ruby smiled. "You could tell some wizard jokes."

"If the queen wanted f-fun," Simon said, "she would have a c-court jester to make her l-laugh, but she doesn't. The m-magic show is m-meant to be serious. But I-I'm a bit clumsy, and my magic is, too! If it goes wrong, the party will be a d-d-disaster!"

"Don't worry," Harry said. "We know a lot about magic. We can help you practise."

Puddle wagged his tail and gave a little "Woof!" as Ruby enthusiastically nodded.

"F-fantastico!" Simon grinned. "Follow me."

He led them up the stone stairs in the gatehouse and out on to the

castle walls. They hurried along the
battlements, then scrambled up a
narrow spiral staircase that went right
to the top of the castle's tallest turret.

"Welcome to the m-magic den,"
Simon said, throwing open the door,
and knocking
over what looked
like an umbrella
stand holding a
long silver stick.

"Whoops!"
he said, as it
clattered to the
ground. "That's

my m-magic wand!" He hurriedly
replaced the wand in its stand.

"Wow!" Ruby said. She and Harry looked in wonder around the candlelit room. Just inside the door was a suit of armour, and on the opposite side to the door there was an enormous stone fireplace decorated with carved dragons. A big round

copper cauldron hung from an iron chain over the glowing embers. The walls were lined with shelves packed with glass bottles full of shimmering neon-coloured liquids. In the middle of the room there was a sturdy wooden table, scorched in places and

covered in spill marks and scratches. And right by it, on a stand, was an enormous old book.

Harry hurried over to it.

"This is the oldest book I've ever seen!" he exclaimed, adjusting his glasses.

"What is it?" Ruby asked excitedly, looking over Harry's shoulder as he brushed away the dust from the gold lettering on the dark red leather cover. She read the name of the book: *Secret Spells and Magnificent Magic*.

Ruby couldn't wait to see what was inside!

# Chapter Four
# Spelling Mistakes

Ruby and Harry carefully turned the pages of *Secret Spells and Magnificent Magic*.

"It's just like my *Big Book of Magic Tricks*," Harry said. "It tells you exactly what to do, step by step."

"That's right. I n-need to follow this spell book until I become a proper wizard," Simon told them.

"Pleeease, show us some of your spells, Simon," Ruby begged.

"I'll t-t-try!" Simon rolled up his sleeves. "What do you g-get if you cross a wizard with an icicle?" he asked mischievously as he took his wand from the stand beside the door. "A c-cold spell!" he said, grinning as Harry and Ruby burst out laughing. Simon whirled round, and accidentally knocked a bottle of dark purple liquid off the shelf with his wand.

"W-whoops!" he exclaimed as

the bottle crashed to the hard stone
floor. A purple puddle spread
across the flagstones, then dissolved
into a whirling cloud that flashed
with lightning as it spiralled up to
the ceiling, then fizzled out like a
firework.

Puddle covered his
eyes with his paws.

49

"Oh dear, that means I can't do the S-Storm Cloud Spell now," Simon murmured, flicking through his spell book. "Ah, yes, here's a good one, he said. "The F-Furry Floating Spell. You can help me with the chant." He pointed to where the spell was written in the book so that Ruby and Harry could read the words with him:

"*Hairy beast with furry coat,*
*Presto! Hocus Pocus –*
*FLOAT!*"

Simon waved his magic wand over Puddle. The little puppy slowly lifted into the air.

"He really is floating." Ruby giggled as Simon pointed at Puddle with his wand and whirled slowly around. Puddle's tail wagged as he soared around Simon's head.

"It must be a trick," Harry said slowly. "I know how it works. Puddle's on a wire attached to Simon's wand." He jumped up and swept his hand across the space between Simon's wand and Puddle. "Nothing's there," Harry said, bewildered. "Then how –"

"It's magic!" Ruby clapped her hands in delight as Simon pointed at Puddle and made a big circle with his wand. Puddle looped the loop, yapping excitedly.

"Now for the t-tricky bit," Simon murmured.

"What's that?" Ruby asked.

"Landing." Simon frowned with concentration. "I have to hold the w-wand just right ... *whoops!*"

The wand clattered to the floor. Ruby tugged her plaits nervously as Puddle dropped like a stone. But, just in time, Simon grabbed the wand and brought Puddle down gently.

"Yip, yip, yip!" Puddle yapped.

Ruby and Harry gave Simon and Puddle a round of applause.

Simon bowed, looking pleased. "And for my n-next spell," he said, "I shall make this suit of armour w-walk!"

"What page is the spell on?" Harry asked, flicking through the book.

"I don't n-need the book for this one," Simon told them. "It goes like this:

*S-suit of armour, hear me talk,*
*Pocus Hocus Presto!*
*WALK!*"

Simon waved his magic wand. The suit of armour fell to the floor with a *craaash!*

Puddle leapt out of the way as the helmet rolled across the floor towards him.

"W-whoops!" Simon said. "I must have said the m-magic words in the wrong order. W-what if I do that at the queen's p-p-p –"

He was interrupted by a sudden fanfare of trumpets from the courtyard.

Harry peered out of a window. "The celebrations are beginning."

"T-time to go," Simon groaned.

"Take the spell book with you," Ruby said. "If you use that, everything will be fine, won't it?"

# Chapter Five
# The Magic Takes Off!

Simon shoved his wand up his sleeve, and grabbed the spell book. Then he dashed out of the magician's den, closely followed by Ruby, Harry and Puddle. His long blue robe wrapped itself round his legs.

"W-w-whoops!" Simon yelled as he *bump, bump, bumped* down the spiral staircase on his bottom. He

landed in a heap, still hanging on
to his precious spell book. Puddle
nudged gently at Simon with his nose.

"W-what do you call a wizard
who lies on the g-ground?" he asked,
smiling and ruffling Puddle's ears.
"Matt!"

Ruby and Harry snorted with
laughter as he struggled to his feet
and readjusted his robe.

They hurried along the battlements towards the gatehouse and clattered down the stone stairs and out into the courtyard. They stood by the catapult and looked around.

Everyone was already seated round the trestle tables that had been set up in a giant rectangle. The tables were piled high with platters of pastries, fruit, meat and tall wobbly jellies, but no one was smiling.

"The people aren't enjoying themselves very much," Ruby commented.

"The queen looks bored, too," said Harry, pointing to the largest table, where the queen was sitting, dressed

in her finest embroidered gown and
gold crown. There was a brass gong
with a wooden hammer, and a giant
birthday cake in front of her. The
cake was in the shape of a fairy-tale
castle, covered in white icing, with
a huge red cherry on the top of the
tallest tower.

Puddle raised his nose into the air and sniffed at the delicious food.

"You're not going to be naughty again, are you?" Ruby asked.

Puddle tilted his head to one side as he looked at her, and wagged his tail.

"Why has no one started eating yet?" Harry asked.

"Th-the acts g-go first," Simon explained. "Th-there are th-three today."

At the top table, the queen looked at her birthday cake and yawned. She drummed her fingers on the brass gong.

"What's the gong for?" Harry asked.

"If the queen gets bored by one of the acts, she hits the gong with the hammer and the act has to stop," Simon said. He gulped. "I hope that doesn't happen to me."

"The entertainment will cheer everyone up," Ruby said, looking for Puddle.

The naughty little puppy was sniffing round the catapult. "Leave that alone!" she told him.

"Are you ready, Simon?" Harry asked.

"I-I'm on l-last," Simon gulped. "My mouth's gone d-dry," he croaked, reaching out for a cup full of lemonade on a nearby table.

"W-whoops!" It slipped from his grasp. Harry picked it up and refilled it from a barrel of lemonade. Simon glugged it down. "Th-thanks. Now it's t-time to take our places!" Simon nervously tapped his spell book with his wand.

"Where shall we sit?" Ruby asked.

"Over th-there!" Simon gestured with the hand holding the spell book. The heavy book slipped out of his hand and landed on the end of the catapult. Then Puddle gave a bark and jumped on the other end.

"No!" shouted Ruby, Harry and Simon. But it was too late.

*Twang!*

*Secret Spells and Magnificent Magic* flew through the air, over the

battlements. There
was a loud *splash!*

"Oh n-no! It's
landed in the
m-moat!"
Simon
turned and raced out of the castle,
under the heavy iron portcullis and
out across the wooden drawbridge.
Ruby, Harry and Puddle sped after
him. They skidded to a halt at the
edge of the deep water. The large
leather-bound book was bobbing up
and down in the middle of the moat.

"It's floating!" Ruby said with a
sigh of relief.

Puddle leapt into the water. His

little legs looked as if he was running as he doggy-paddled towards the spell book. Suddenly, three enormous swans sailed into view. The huge birds swam towards the book and began to peck at it with their sharp orange beaks.

"What are they doing?" Simon asked.

"They think they can eat the book," Ruby murmured. "It'll sink if they keep pecking at it."

Puddle doggy-paddled towards the swans. "Woof, woof, woof!" he barked.

The huge white birds stopped pecking at the book and looked at the little puppy. Then, all at once, they

stretched out their long necks and
began to beat their powerful wings.

*Ssssss!* they hissed fiercely.

"They're going to attack Puddle!"
Harry yelled.

# Chapter Six
# Puddle Saves the Day

"We have to distract them!" Ruby cried. Her plaits swung as she raced back into the castle and sneakily grabbed a handful of bread rolls from one of the tables. She thrust them at Simon and Harry.

"Tear them up and throw them to the swans," she panted. They hurled a snowstorm of breadcrumbs between

Puddle and the fierce-looking birds. Ruby breathed a sigh of relief as the swans folded their wings and began to gobble up the bread.

Puddle grabbed the corner of the book in his teeth. Then he turned and doggy-paddled back to the bank.

"W-well done, Puddle!" Simon said, leaning over the water to take the book from Puddle. Ruby and Harry had to grab hold of Simon's cloak to stop him falling in the water. As Simon triumphantly lifted up the dripping book, something plopped out of his sleeve and sank in the moat.

Puddle leapt out of the moat and shook himself from nose to tail,

sending a shower of water droplets
all over them. Ruby laughed as she
wrung the water from her plaits.

Harry dried his glasses on his sleeve.

"Is the spell book OK?" he asked Simon, pushing his glasses back on to his nose.

Simon opened *Secret Spells and Magnificent Magic*. The paper was all mushy and ink was running down the pages.

"I-I can't read any of the words!" he said. "I-I'll use my wand to d-dry it out."

He stuck
his hand up
his sleeve.
"I've lost
my wand!"
he wailed,
dropping
the book.
"There's no
way I can do any
m-magic now!"

Ruby looked at Harry.

"We can help you put on a great show without a magic wand," she told Simon.

"You c-can?" Simon asked in disbelief.

Harry stared at Ruby over his glasses. "They don't have paper cups in a medieval castle," he whispered. "And we don't know where they keep the marbles."

Puddle tilted his head.

"Woof! Woof!" He dashed towards the castle.

"This is no time to be naughty,"

Ruby groaned as they raced after him. She could hardly believe her eyes. The little puppy was trotting between the table legs towards the queen's table.

When the queen's back was turned, Puddle leapt up and grabbed the cherry from the top of her birthday cake!

He scooted back to them, with his nose covered in cream.

"Drop!" Ruby ordered. Puddle spat out the cherry at her feet.

"That looks just like a big marble,"

Harry said thoughtfully. "Now all we need is the cup with a hole in it." He picked up a cup from a nearby table, and began to tap a hole in the bottom of it with the end of a spoon.

Ruby clapped her hands. "We've got everything we need to put on a spectacular show!" she told Simon excitedly.

# Chapter Seven
# Spectacular Arts

Three trumpeters raised their trumpets and blew a fanfare.

"T-time for the f-first act!" Simon whispered.

"Fabulous Ferdinand!" the leading trumpeter announced.

A man with a bird of prey perched on his arm took his place on a small platform in front of the queen.

"The bird is a falcon," Harry told Ruby as Fabulous Ferdinand threw the bird into the air. It hovered above the courtyard.

Fabulous Ferdinand whistled, and the bird plummeted down towards Simon.

"W-whoops!" Simon ducked as the falcon swooped away with his wizard's hat.

"Fabulous Ferdinand is a falconer," Harry whispered as the falcon flew back to perch on the man's arm. "He's trained the falcon. It takes a lot of skill and patience."

Fabulous Ferdinand gave his falcon a piece of meat, then everyone clapped politely as the bird put the hat back on Simon's head. Simon squished it into place. It looked even more crumpled than before.

The queen picked up the wooden hammer and stood up. "Falcons and hats!" she announced. "I've seen it all before." She walloped the gong with the hammer.

*GOOONNNG!*

"Go home, Fabulous Ferdinand!" cried the queen. "Give me something new!"

The trumpeters lifted their
trumpets and blew another fanfare.

"Lanky Longbow!" the leading
trumpeter announced.

A very tall archer stepped forward
and set up his target at one end of the
rectangle of tables.
The people behind
it hurriedly moved
out of the way as the
archer walked to the
opposite end,
turned, and
pulled back
his bow. In quick
succession, he fired
off five arrows.

83

*Wheee!* The arrows whizzed through the air and landed *thwack, thwack, thwack, thwack, thwack!*

"He only hit the target with one!" Ruby exclaimed. "Where did the other arrows go?"

Harry pushed his glasses up his nose. "He hit the bullseye five times," he told Ruby. "Each arrow split the one before it. That's amazing."

The crowd gave Lanky Longbow another polite round of applause.

The queen stood up with the hammer in her hand. "When you've seen one arrow," she grumbled loudly, "you've seen them all. There's no way you can top that, Lanky Longbow, so you might as well go home."

The queen raised her hammer. *GOOONNNG!* went the brass gong.

"She's very hard to please," Ruby whispered to Harry.

The trumpeters sounded another fanfare.

"M-my t-t-turn." Simon was shaking so hard that his wizard hat fell off.

"The Great Magnifico is unwell,"

the leading trumpeter announced. "In his place we have the wizard-in-training . . ." He looked at Simon and raised his eyebrows. "Your wizard name?" he asked.

"I-I haven't g-g-got one!" Simon muttered, crumpling his wizard's hat between his hands.

Ruby stood on tiptoe and whispered something in the trumpeter's ear.

"Simon Spectacular!" the trumpeter announced as Simon pulled on his crumpled hat. Simon, Ruby, Harry and Puddle stepped on to a small stage in front of the queen's table. Ruby tugged at her plaits for luck.

"Simon Spectacular will make this magically disappear!" she announced, holding up the cherry.

Harry handed Simon the cup, being careful not to let anyone see the hole in the bottom.

With a flourish, Simon dropped the cherry into the cup.

"*Sh-Sh-Shazzzam!*" he shouted, waving his hand over the top.

"*Ta-da!*" Ruby held her arms wide, as Simon tipped over the cup. She held her breath. Nothing fell out. The cherry had disappeared. The trick had worked!

"Woof!" Puddle barked, wagging his tail.

The crowd applauded as Simon carefully handed the cup to Harry.

"And now Simon Spectacular

will magic back the cherry!" Ruby announced. "*Ta-da!*"

Simon stretched out his hand towards the queen, and pretended to pull the cherry out of her crown.

"At last, something new!" the queen declared, clapping her hands. "Well done, Simon Spectacular."

Simon swept off his hat and bowed low. Then he leaned over the table and stuck the cherry back on the queen's birthday cake, covering his hat in cream, and knocking over a plate full of sausages. A string of sausages dangled over the edge of the queen's table.

Puddle sniffed the air. His ears pricked up.

"He's going to spoil the act," Ruby hissed as Simon wedged his sticky hat back on. "Get him!"

Simon, Harry and Ruby threw themselves at the naughty puppy as he launched himself towards the queen's sausages.

# Chapter Eight
# Magic Moments

"Woof!" Puddle barked in surprise
as Ruby, Simon and Harry collided
with him, just as he grabbed the
string of sausages.

They fell back on to the little stage.
Simon staggered to his feet. His
crumpled, cream-covered wizard's
hat was squashed down over his
nose and the string of sausages was

wrapped round his neck. A naughty little puppy was swinging from one end, wagging his tail so hard that it was a blur.

Simon looked down at Puddle. Ruby could see that the wizard's eyes were sparkling with mischief.

"What have you got there, Puddle?" Simon asked. "Is it a l-lead so I can take you for a walk?"

He waggled the string of sausages, which made Puddle kick his legs excitedly. The crowd giggled.

"It's not a l-lead," said Simon, scratching his head. He turned to the crowd. "What c-can it be?"

"A snake!" shouted the queen,

clapping her hands.

Simon gave a loud gasp, pretending to be scared, and the crowd chuckled. "Tee hee hee!"

"A-argh!" Simon cried, pretending to wrestle with the string of sausages. "A rare s-sausage snake has got me in its coils."

"Ha ha ha!" the crowd laughed.

Ruby looked at Simon. He was loving it! There was a big grin on his face.

"And now, the sausage snake will magically shrink!" Simon announced confidently as a section of the string of sausages came away in Puddle's jaws.

"*Hocus Pocus Presto!*" Simon waved his hands over Puddle while the naughty little puppy gobbled the sausages down.

"I give you the Spectacular Disappearing Sausage Act!" Simon swept off his hat and bowed.

The crowd rose to their feet, cheering and clapping. The queen wiped tears of laughter from her eyes as she stood up from the table and joined Simon on the little stage.

"Simon Spectacular," she gasped. "You have made the whole castle happy! We need a jester. You'd be perfect for the job. Will you accept?"

"Yes, please!" said Simon,

kneeling before the queen.

"You will need a jester's hat," the queen announced, removing Simon's battered wizard hat. "I shall order a new one to be made."

"Until then, I'll wear the sausages," Simon chuckled, wrapping them round his head.

Puddle's ears twitched as everyone laughed and cheered.

"This is the most fun I've ever had at one birthday!" the queen laughed.

Simon blushed. "I couldn't have done it without the help of my new friends," he told her. "May I introduce Ruby, Harry – and Puddle!"

Ruby and Harry bowed as Puddle

stood up on his hind legs.

"Delighted to meet you," the queen said.

Puddle yapped happily. Then he slowly began to run in circles round Ruby and Harry.

"We have to go home now," Ruby told Simon. "It's time for us to do our disappearing trick."

"Goodbye!" Ruby and Harry called as Puddle ran faster and faster. Everything was becoming a blur.

"And now, for my grand finale, I shall make my new friends disappear!" Ruby heard Simon tell the queen as the castle dissolved into the sunshine.

In an instant, they were back outside Grandad's cottage. Bright rays of sunlight were breaking through the clouds.

"All that food and we didn't even

get a single bite," Ruby said. "My tummy is hungry. I hope Grandad has made some more of his delicious biscuits for tea."

Puddle scampered ahead as they hurried towards the cottage door. Something was lying in the middle of the garden path. It was a long, thin silver stick.

"That's Simon's wand!" Harry exclaimed as Puddle grabbed it in his mouth. The little puppy's tail wagged happily as he dropped the wand at Ruby's feet.

"Thanks, Puddle." Ruby stooped to pick up the wand. When she stood up, Puddle had disappeared.

"Just like magic!" Harry murmured.

"Puddle will be back next time it rains." Ruby smiled, opening the door to Grandad's cottage.

"There's a plate of biscuits on the kitchen table," Harry called. "Grandad must be a mind-reader!"

"Maybe Grandad's a wizard, too." Ruby laughed as she closed the door. She was already looking forward to their next rainy day adventure!

Can't wait to find out
what Puddle will do next?
Then read on! Here is the first
chapter from Puddle's seventh
adventure, Pirate Surprise...

# Pirate Surprise

"*Brrp brrp, brrp brrp, brrp brrp, brrrrrrrrp!*" Ruby blew through the reeds she had pressed between her thumbs, making a trumpet sound. "Announcing Queen Ruby!" she shouted. Her voice echoed around Grandad's pond.

"What about me?" Harry asked. He smiled and gazed proudly at the model sailing ship he was holding.

"Ooops. Sorry," Ruby said and then shouted, "and announcing the Queen's Master Ship Builder, Harry!"

The cousins' wellies squelched in the mud as they marched to the pond's edge and set the ship down. Harry took out his compass and unrolled the map of the pond that he had made earlier.

"We are ready to launch the boat," Ruby said in her best queenly voice.

"She's a ship," Harry said.

"Who's a ship?" Ruby asked.

"My model, she's a sea-going ship. Not a boat," Harry explained. "Ships are bigger and have three or more masts. Just remember, a boat can fit in a ship, but a ship can't fit in a boat."

"But yours can fit in a bathtub?" Ruby rolled her eyes. "Never mind. We are ready to launch the ship. Now for the fun bit where we christen it with the bottle." Ruby held up a bottle of fizzy drink, shook it and started to unscrew the cap.

"Wait!" Harry exclaimed. "I need to check the course one more time." He scanned his map.

*Splat!* A large drop of rain plopped on to the map. Then another drop fell, then another. The pond was now rippling with raindrops.

Ruby and Harry shouted together, "Hooray, it's raining!"

*Come on Puddle*, Ruby thought. *Where will we go this time?* They scouted around for Puddle but there was no sign of the naughty puppy. Puddle magically appeared whenever it started raining and took Ruby and Harry on amazing adventures. *Oh no, maybe he's not coming*, Ruby wondered.

Suddenly they heard a rustling in the reeds behind them, and *whump* – out bounded Puddle, leaping high into the air above the pond.

"Woof!" Puddle yipped as he landed in the water with a terrific splash. The wave he made pushed

Harry's ship on to the mud and soaked the cousins through. Ruby slipped and her thumb knocked against the top of the fizzy drink, which was still in her hand.

"Ooops!" she squealed as it popped its top and sprayed all over Harry.

"Yuck!" Harry said, wiping his sticky glasses.

"Naughty Puddle," Ruby said through her laughter. "You scared us and you could have sunk Harry's ship!"

Puddle leapt out of the pond and started to shake himself dry.

"Puddle!" Harry shouted as his glasses got splashed once more.

Puddle ran in and out of Harry's legs and wagged his tail.

"At least the water washed off the fizzy drink," Ruby said, giggling.

Harry smiled at the playful puppy. "You are the naughtiest puppy I know. Oh no, my map!" Harry held up the soggy paper. He put the compass safely in his pocket.

Puddle yapped and dashed down Grandad's garden path. He scampered among the puddles then circled a large one near the garden gate. Ruby and Harry raced over.

"I guess this is the one," Ruby said, getting ready to hop into it with Puddle. "Come on. Let's all go together this time," she suggested, holding out her hand to Harry.

"Are you sure we'll fit?" Harry asked.

Ruby gripped his hand and tugged on her plaits for luck. "One way to find out."

"OK," Harry said. He took a deep breath. "Here goes!"

And they all jumped into the puddle and disappeared with an enormous splash.

\*\*\*

To find out what happens next, get your copy of PIRATE SURPRISE today!

# Ballet Show Mischief

Go on a beautiful ballet adventure
with Puddle, Ruby and Harry.

The children are
whisked away to a
wonderful ballet
show, but the shy
ballerina has stage
fright. The show
must go on! Will
Puddle be able to
find a solution?

Find out in BALLET SHOW MISCHIEF...

# Puddle
## the naughtiest puppy

# Rainforest
# Hide and Seek

Have you ever wanted to see a rainforest?

Puddle uses his
magic to take Ruby
and Harry through
a puddle and into an
incredible animal
adventure. Things
keep going missing
in the rainforest
– can Puddle find
out why?

Find out in RAINFOREST HIDE AND SEEK…

# Puddle
## the naughtiest puppy

# Dragon Dance

Join Puddle, Ruby and Harry on their new adventure in Chinatown!

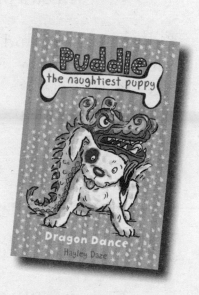

Li wants to make his grandad proud by appearing in the Chinese festival. Can Puddle and the children help him to get Lucky the dragon to dance?

Find out in DRAGON DANCE...

# Pirate Surprise

Can you imagine what it's like to
sail on a pirate ship?

Ruby and Harry find
out – when Puddle
takes them on an
amazing adventure
on the high seas!
Captain Redbeard
has a bad case of the
hiccups! Will Puddle
be able to cure him?

Find out in PIRATE SURPRISE...
Coming soon!

# Animal Antics

Join Puddle, Ruby and Harry
at the Safari Rescue Park!

All the animals
have problems they
need to overcome
before they can be
released into the
wild. Will Puddle
be able to help the
monkey who is
afraid of heights?

Find out in ANIMAL ANTICS…
Coming soon!

## A Place to Rest

Hi, everyone! It's Ruby and Harry with Puddle the puppy here. Wow, we are pretty tired after that adventure! Luckily, today our friends at **Dogs Trust** – the UK's largest dog charity – are going to explain how important it is for a dog to have somewhere of its own to rest, sleep and have some quiet time.

When we are tired we can go to our bedrooms, get tucked in and go to sleep. Dogs need to be able to do the same – to go to a special place where they can be left alone for a while.

But make sure that you don't leave your dog alone for too long in its own space – check that it is feeling okay.

Always remember, Puddle is a magical dog, while real dogs and puppies are living animals who need a lot of care, love and attention.

## Dog Beds:

- While they don't need their own bedrooms, dogs do need to have their own beds!
- There are many types of beds available for different dogs; some are hard, some are soft — it really depends on what your best doggy friend prefers!
- Whatever the bed, remember that all dogs need a favourite blanket to keep them warm!

If you had a dog, where do you think the best place for its bed would be in your house?

Or if you have a dog at the moment, where does it sleep?

Congratulations – you now know about how important it is for a dog to have somewhere to rest! See you next time, when we will be talking about a dog's play-time.

Remember, "A dog is for life, not just for Christmas®" Dogs Trust has 18 Rehoming Centres around the UK and Ireland. To find out more please go to:
 www.dogstrust.org.uk
For more fun and games please go to:
www.learnwithdogs.co.uk

# Medieval Muddle!

Ruby and Harry had an amazing adventure at the medieval castle. Which of these are things you would expect to find in a castle? Point to the things that don't belong.

# Jigsaw Jumble!

Look carefully at the picture of Ruby, Harry and Puddle with Simon. It has several pieces missing! Can you work out which of the jigsaw pieces on this page fits into each space?

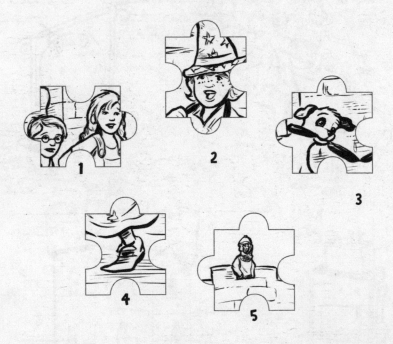

Answers on the next page

Answers to puzzles:
Medieval Muddle: Ruby's toy Teddy, Harry's robot Chips, trainers
Jigsaw Jumble: 1-B, 2-D, 3-C, 4-E, 5-A

For more magical adventures, come and play with Puddle at

www.puddlethepuppy.com

Use this special code to get extra-special games and free stuff at puddlethepuppy.com

WAND